DEAR DREAM

LIVE IT OR LOSE IT!

PREETI AGARWAL

Contents

To the beautiful dream which resides within us!

Acknowledgements

I am deeply grateful to all my readers, whose encouragement has given me the energy to pour my thoughts into this story.

I wish for all my readers to achieve their dreams and aspirations, and I hope this book makes a positive difference in their lives.

I dedicate this book to my children, Sneha and Ojusav, who inspire me, allow me to soar, follow my heart, and fulfil my dream of authoring this book.

I thank God for giving me the strength and inspiration to create this work.

My heartfelt thanks go to my parents, supporters, and well-wishers for their unwavering support throughout my writing journey.

I am also grateful to the editor, printer, and publisher for bringing this book to its destination.

Preface

Do not cage yourself in an unheard room.
Come out of your shell,
Write down the story of your dream!
Create your characters.
Let them glow and shine!
So that glitter spread everywhere!
Let us get inside the dream,
A sacred place where there is no sinner, no winner.
Where you can share your sorrow and happiness.
Just you, your desires, and goals to grow.
Let's get inside the dream,
where voices are free.
To tell the truth,
to fill it with colours of hope!
Let us get inside the dream,
Touch your heart to feel the core!
Where silence resides, emotions guide to flow.
Let's get inside the dream!

Dear Dream, it was just a thought, a dream that has been converted into reality... a book!!

I was in a dilemma - how could I reach the enormous number of people with my insight?

What should be the form of my wisdom about dreams? A short story, a blog, an article, or an essay that leads others to venture into the dream journey. I started writing and creating stories with this topic and finally, I am here with my final output...a book!!

I dream that I will pen down this book with the intention that it touches millions of hearts.

PREFACE

I authored this book to raise a voice that was left unheard.

When we sleep, our dreams determine the unhidden desires which have lost their shine,

sights that had forgotten their fascination,

Secrets that are ready to be revealed.

Dreams for us are like

Singer with a song

Musician with music

Writer with a story.

Painter with colours.

Let us indulge in dreams and create our illuminating world!

Listen to the mystical symphony of dreams,

A mingle with its riveting hidden sights,

With jingle of an enthralling life vision!!

So, my dear readers, immerse yourself in this book to create your dream, your REALITY.

Character List

Part I

Scientist Frederick, Oneirologist.
Emily, Patient 1
Patrick, Patient 2
Stephanie, Patient 3.
Rebecca, Emily's Mother
James, Emily's Father
Joseph, Dream interpreter
Jeffrey, Heist Leader
Selina, Stephanie's mother.
Athena, the Child
Sam, Dream Architect
Roger, Dream Weaver
Parker, Dream Catcher
Barner, Dream Alchemist
Larson, Dream Chronicle
Katie, Dream Detective

Part 2

Samuel Wilson, Contestant 1
Eddie Smith, Contestant 2
Henry Brown, Contestant 3
Fiona Greens, Contestant 4
Hannah Collins, Contestant 5
Olivia Collins, Contestant 6
Amelia Collins, Contestant 7
Charlotte Brookes, Contestant 8

CHAPTER ONE

ASTOUNDING SHOW IN THE TOWN

This was the time of December, lush green trees were laden with snow, creating calm surroundings engulfed with crispy and chilling winter. A silent windy night, where vacant roads were frosting with the shimmering streetlights which adore the beauty of hidden silvery moon with their luminous glow.

The town hall was beaming with profuse chandeliers, backed by a jampacked audience.

It has a major attraction as the biggest show of the country with intricate features is going to be held in Nottingham Hall. An enormous number of people have gathered to attend the show.

The stage was beautifully decorated with exquisite flowers and colourful hangings. The centre stage was adorned with a red-coloured carpet with splendid blue side borders to exalt the stage performance of the participants.

The judges were sitting just in front of the stage to hear and evaluate the competitors.

What is the distinctive feature of the event? Readers, can you guess?

It was the Biggest Dreamer Award!

There are several categories of prizes associated with this award.

First time, this award was designed to honour the biggest dreamer of the country.

Every participant must fill out the form mentioning their dream by answering multiple questions to apply for this award in the first round.

A nominal fee is charged from various participants, and the results are published in the country newspaper.

The Capacity of the hall was around more than twenty thousand people. The splendour and grandeur beauty of the hall was alluring as multicoloured light fascinates the large chunks of the crowd. A cultural programme was also organised in between the various award presentations to entertain the crowd.

Every contestant must demonstrate how big his or her dream is. They must narrate it in story form or enact the various incidents that occurred in the dream fulfilment.

Finally, the show started!!

The chief guest of the event is a renowned Counsellor Marie, eminent Scientist Frederick, and illustrious Educationalist Robert.

The guests were greeted with a green plant as a welcome gesture by the host of the event.

The various categories of the awards:
The Biggest Dreamer
The First Runner-Up

The Second Runner-Up

The Visionary Dreamer

The criterion for choosing the biggest dreamer in each category is the one who faces the maximum challenges in pursuing the dream and works for the betterment of future generations.

The dream pageant was a hunt for the ideal dreamer of the country with the intention to inspire people, so they work towards fulfilling their dreams.

Scientist Frederick was excited to judge the best dreamer as his whole life was based on the concept of dream evaluation.

He had a vast and profound knowledge about this topic.

The event started as the first participant moved towards the centre of the stage and spoke a few lines on a dream:

I love to dream

Dream of hope

Dream of growth

Dream of happiness

Dream of joy

The dream that amazes me.

The dream that illuminates me and lets me shine like stars.

I love to dream.

Dream of challenges develops perseverance,

A strength to overcome my weakness.

A supportive friend in the tempest of obstacles

I love to dream.

My dream combines my passion with my compassion.

It is a world where I learn to metamorphose my life.

Every day, I have a dream with

new thoughts

new insights and

new aspirations

I love to dream.

The crowd applauded the participant for the beautiful narration of the dream.

As the programme proceeds, Scientist Frederick gets back into his flashback story.

CHAPTER TWO

The Man who Discovered Dream Formula

It was a big scientific laboratory where experiment was conducted to detect the colour of new solution, all were gathered at one place, waiting for the astonishing result.

When the solution turned blue, all the assistants get confused and startle, they were expecting pink colour of the solution.

A tall man, robust body, white beard, a stern face with protruding eyes called one of his interns and guided him to use a different process. This tall man is Scientist Frederick Cruz who is a brilliant, wise, sagacious, and quick-witted person who discovered the basic nature of the solution and assessed the actual problem.

Last night when he was working late in his lab, he discovered a formula that can convert dreams into reality. He decided to share this formula related to dreams with the person who genuinely needed it and was backed by one condition: it can be used for a good purpose. If by any chance this formula is misused, then his/her dream would be converted into a nightmare.

He was quite inquisitive about dream theory. He was always curious about the concept of dreams. There were various questions which used to linger in his mind.

What is a dream?

Where do they come from and where do they go?

How can I convert a dream into reality?

What is the hidden truth residing within every dream?

Mystery associated with dreams and how to cope with dream vision?

When can I truly be able to understand the voyage of dreams?

As he discovered this formula connected to dreams, he acquired the ability to conquer the dream vision and leave his physical body to travel to a different realm of existence.

Scientists created a team of experts to fulfil people's dreams into reality and its associated factors.

The members of the dream team are:

1. Sam, the Dream Architect, who constructs good dreams for the needy for their better future.

2. Roger, the Dream Weaver, who found the dreams of others from scratch to end, to create a space and niche connection between dream and reality.

3. Parker - the Dream Catcher, an assistant of Scientist Frederick who developed the ability to catch the dreams of a person.

4. Barner - the Dream Alchemist who is an expert in solving the quest of dreams.

5. Larson - the Dream Chronicles, who turn into dream characters and solve puzzles and mysteries related to dreams.

6. Katie - the Dream Detective who solves the crime-related cases behind the dream.

Scientist Frederick heads the team as Dream Walker who walks and enters others' dreams to find the truth. He captures the dreams of others to eliminate the dark evil inside them.

After he discovered the formula along with his expert team, he became popular in the country. Thousands of people approached him, but he used a lottery system for the neediest people, and the lucky one gets a chance to turn their dream into reality.

According to him-

Focus your energy on your dream!

It will magnetically come to you.

It attracts what you dream with the magic formula!

He put a slogan in front of his entrance.

Choose your Dream! Change your LIFE!!

CHAPTER THREE

Emily's Dialogue with Scientist Frederick

Scientist Frederick saw Emily, a pretty girl with stunning features, golden hair falling on her face as dawn as the base of sheer.

He enquired to her, "Why she is here?"

She narrated the whole story to him.

Emily's father died when she was a teenager. After his demise, the dream was the only place where Emily met her father. Emily has an emotional connection with her father and whenever she perceives him in her dream, she has a desire to find the cause of why he appears in her dream.

Emily woke up early in the morning for the past few months. She struggles daily with the recurring appearances of her father in dreams and finds it difficult to solve this puzzle. A quest always haunts her when she wakes up. It torments her, a relationship issue which is still not resolved.

Emily told her mother, Rebecca, about father meeting in a dream. Her mother was quite amused, and she enquired what made her anxious when she saw that dream. She answered, "Something peculiar, dad wants to convey some hidden secret yet not disclosed."

One day, through an acquaintance, they came to know about the dream interpreter Joseph who could understand the dream visions. Both the daughter and mother went to the fellow Joseph. He was an awful guy and an avaricious person. He took a large amount of money from Rebecca and tormented Emily. But somehow, with God's grace, they were protected from his ill feelings and selfish motives.

Later, they came to know about the scientist who has a magic formula to catch, weave, and find solutions for dreams and their origin.

Emily initially tried to find the truth behind the dream. She just murmured one night when she was full of anguish and not able to sleep.

"Dear Dream,

Where are you?

I searched for you in the cool breeze...

I wandered through the lush green garden to find you...

I hunted you under my soft velvet pillow.

But you vanished...

I slept night after night!

...waiting for you!

You are like a rat with no trace of yours,

Dear dream,

Where are you?

In my childhood days,

You always walk beside me...

Giving daily doses of inspiration with stories to grow.

You solve so many questions in my tiny world.

Dear Dream,
Where are you?
You are my inborn doctor who freed me from grief,
Provide me peace of mind!
Here is a mystery at the core, unresolved problems.
Yet you enriched my soul by bringing positive sights.
Just solve the quest of my life.
Dear Dream,
Where are you?
Just waiting for you...
As sunlight approaches,
Your shimmer spread on my heart with the fragrance of joy,
I admire when you are alive with me.
Dear Dream,
Where are you?
Let me come out of false promises and adhere to real ties.
Give me sunshine of hope,
So that I venture into the world of growth
Dear Dream,
Where are you?
Just ready,
To catch hold of you!

Emily was quite dismayed with the behaviour of Joseph and finally decided to meet Scientist Frederick. When she went for a consultation, he reassured her. It seems every cloud has a silver lining.

CHAPTER FOUR

PATRICK VISITS SCIENTIST FREDERICK

Home Minister of External Affairs called an urgent meeting for the puzzle of the robbery case. He received a call from Scientist Frederick about the dream of Patrick who saw the robbery. It was Jeffrey and the gang, a notorious group who had planned to rob the World Bank. They have a record of conducting various heists in the country.

Although security is tight with twenty-five members to take care of the treasury room. The minister always believes the word of the scientist as he is true to his words.

Patrick, an adorable child full of curiosity and desire to grow, had a small face with twinkling eyes, hair scattered all over his face, and an enchanting smile; none could forget his innocent eyes. He was quite eager to ask questions about every notion from his childhood days.

When he was five years old, he dreamed of a superpower who fought with monsters. Patrick often recollects his dream as it gives him inspiration to be fearless in his daily life. He had a strong imagination, and it inculcated the spirit of power and courage in his adulthood.

One night, thieves attacked his house. It was a dark night, silence opened its wings, all house locked with just streetlights, spreading their vision to move on the path. Patrick town was safe and secure, but the district has a history of thieves who stay near the forest area and loot the villagers.

Patrick has a family of four people - his mother, father, himself, and little sister. They have a happy family with limited income. His parents are well-bred and contented with their life. As a daily ritual at night, his mother used to narrate a story to him.

His mother never forgets how he narrated the story of super powerful hero Neil the Sailor. He said, "Mother, it was an amazing experience! How can someone be so strong that he kills the monsters without any help?"

Patrick's mother always asks him to be motivated by the dream; she knows deep down her son wants to be like him.

He started writing in his school diary and collecting dream memories. His sister wants to dance even though she cannot walk. Patrick wants to help his little sister with tiny joyful activities.

One dark night, the thieves burst into his house and forced his parents to surrender their valuables. Patrick was so terrified that he remained silent, unsure of how to confront the thieves who brandished knives and had their faces covered.

A few minutes later, he innocently asked one thief, "I am very thirsty! Can I drink water with my bottle?" He ran towards his room as the thief consented. Patrick hid himself behind the curtains and rang the toy of a mock police siren whose sound could be heard from a long distance.

As thieves heard the loud sound of the siren, they thought that the local police had arrived and would arrest them, so the thieves ran away. That day, Patrick started believing in the power of a superhero dream. People praised his quick and intelligent task of ringing the false police siren.

He visited the scientist and discussed all about his dream.

CHAPTER FIVE

STEPHANIE'S DESIRE TO TELL THE TRUTH

When Emily contacted Scientist Frederick, she talked about the expertise of the scientist to her distant cousin Stephanie. She discussed the various issues pertaining to dreams.

Stephanie was a girl of split personality. The life of Stephanie was quite complex. Her father had the habit of gambling and drinking. He used to come home late at night and ill-treat her mother, Selina. Stephanie had an adorable face, bright eyes, softly rounded cheeks, a slightly dimpled chin, a slim body structure with blue bruises on her hands. The bruises depicted the cruelty of her father to everyone.

Stephanie was a clever girl and wanted to be free from these atrocities. Her mother Selina pays her school fees through her coaching classes. Stephanie used to compose small poems to subdue her grief. She realises that she has a two-sided personality - one which is gloomy, and the other one is cheerful. Her daily routine involves going with Selina to a few homes where she tutored children of rich and affluent families.

One night, she saw in her dream that one student, a small girl named Athena, was abducted by unknown people near where her mother goes for tuition classes. Stephnie used to play with her. She got confused and scared to discuss her dream, which pertained to that incident. She felt that nobody was going to believe her.

Stephanie ventured into a dream with a thought:
Oh! Dream,
hold my hand!
To direct my path
Find me a dream of realness behind my twinkling eyes.
Oh! Dream, hold my hand!
Just embrace me under the cover of the silent night.
I am mesmerised by you!!
How do you express such emotions?
How do you resolve so many issues?
How can you help us uncover the hidden
secret?
Oh! Dream, hold my path.
as sleep forsakes my eyes,
To find the actual criminal,
To disclose the tragic incident.
To protect the missing child.
Oh! Dream, hold my hand!!
She scheduled an appointment with Scientist Frederick.

CHAPTER SIX

Dream Analysis in Motion

Scientist Frederick prepared a schedule for every client. He created a guide to direct the dreamers. He does Oneiric study to reach the depth of dreams. His diaries have details of every client's dream as several dreamers remember their dream and few forget, so he has interpersonal guidebook to understand the dream.

His dream diary was the treasure trove of dreams which great insights. How dreams can be manifested, how affirmations are spoken to create happy dreams.

In ancient times, there was a book named Dream Lunaries based on the current phase of the Moon, which was used by various researchers. Scientist Frederick utilizes these dream lunaries and mantic alphabets to analyse dream scenarios.

Scientist Frederick figures out the process of dream conversion into reality through an experiment that led to the creation of a formula. He put a lot of labour into discovering the formula connected to the dream. The scientist woke up early in the morning and wrote notes to put them into reality. It is a REM sleep - linked with a dream where oneiric vision appears in the night.

The scientist initiated the dream evaluation process. He asked Emily to choose a dream. She always wants to find the truth behind her father's dream.

He asked, "Emily! Run through your thought process numerous times; it will stay with you. Imagine your dream again and again; take it to your desired thought. Script your dream into a tiny story. Prepare your own journal of what you see in a dream.

Any symbol, any place, and any characters mentioned, if any text reads it, any signal visualises it, read numerous times and visualise it repeatedly.

Her dream unsettles her, and she deliberately wishes to hear what her father desires to tell her.

The scientist took his clients for dream incubation, which means a pre-sleep practice of generating a dream to provide insight about the topic. The sight of the dream became a revelation for the true feelings of her father.

Scientist Frederick asked her to frame questions straight and concise. These questions link the marks for him. He told Emily to write questions in her dream journal before she visits the dream reiteration process - a kind of daily rehearsal for her.

He said, "When you get around to dreaming, jot down everything you have seen and share it with me. I will reveal the true picture - the themes, major symbols, and all the relevant information."

CHAPTER SEVEN

PROCESS CONTINUES

Scientist Frederick was quite near to the true picture of Emily's dream. He placed objects related to the dream near Emily in every session.

Her father's photos, watch, and the certificate of profession were set in the dream session room. The fragrance of her father's perfume was suffused around the room.

The dream journey is aligned with this concept. The childhood birthday presents and books given by her father were also positioned in the Dream incubation room. A dream altar was created with candles, fresh flowers, crystals, seashells, and pictures that create dream intentions.

Last and least, he told Emily, "Keep 10 minutes of silence and bring the image to your mind, write it down to give a clear and concise picture. Do certain affirmations to reach a concrete result." It took two months for the scientist to come out with Emily's answers. He enquired of Emily about oneiric visions. He wants to find the truth of questions alluring her to gain awareness in the conscious mind. He used video recording of Emily for dream evaluation.

It was a challenge for Emily to remember the dream clearly. After using the dream formula, she used active imagination where she remembered the current dream and had communication with her father.

He used various strategies and collated reports to reach the conclusion.

Scientist Frederick made Emily so fascinated by the dream incubation process that she authored a beautiful poem on its experience. She waits for every night to rejuvenate and enter the splendid odyssey of dreams.

"Dream! Dream! Dream!"
Let me live one day of your life,
Join me on my journey,
To surmount my fears,
The tears, torment come and go...
after every night,
As you hold my hands,
I have found my life as I get you...
...to live my life.
I wake up every day,
I sleep every day,
with hope of a beautiful dream of truth,
A reality, it grows,
A desire to fulfil,
A breath I want to inhale and exhale.
As I have you in my life!
Dream!
Dream! Dream!
Let me live one day of your life!

CHAPTER EIGHT

PATRICK'S DREAM EVALUATION

Meanwhile, Scientist Frederick started his tests for Patrick. He reviewed what he had told and found it difficult to reach a conclusion in one day.

He ordered Patrick to create a dream journal where he wrote every aspect of the dream he remembers. Any symbols, alphabets surrounding it, just mention them.

Scientist Frederick took the help of his team Parker, the Dream Catcher who catches and controls the dream. They navigate Patrick's dream to make a connection between dream and reality. He developed confidence in himself so he can visualise his dream properly.

He asked, "Just jot down the scene. It is not necessary for you to write in order. Do not analyse it, just leave it to me; I will interpret it. You can draw the images you have seen. Any colour you notice, tell me. You can mention any objects, their shape, for example, a key-passcode, passwords."

If you speak of what you have seen, then only can we come close to the actual vision. At night, you can stay in my laboratory. If you feel comfortable, I can video record as it depicts the true picture.

When you are at home, you will not be able to tell the actual components."

One day, at home, Patrick gets up in a hurry to speak his mind and wrote down his last night's dream. As five minutes passed, he started forgetting his dream vision... Sometimes, he is as blank as fog, due to which Frederick insisted on repeated imaging which can bring forth the dream that needed the mystery to be solved.

When he stayed at the scientist's laboratory, he gave him a dream journal which has motivational quotes on it. A spiral-bound diary with colourful images in the corner. It has numerous blank pages with lines on a few pages.

Scientist Frederick told him, "It is a two-sided journal where on one side you jot down your thoughts. On the other side, I will write the outcome." Along with the title of the dream, he asked him to hang a dream catcher above his bed so that he feels protected and secure.

Patrick was happy as now he felt that he could communicate with dreams and would become a superhero. He started remembering the lines told by his father:

Stick to your dream...

So many opportunities.

So many options, but one dream to grow!

Never lose hope to grow,

Just bloom into a flower with a seed of a dream to glow,

Stick to your dreams!

CHAPTER NINE

Stephanie Opening Up

As soon as Emily gave the address to Stephanie, she reached Scientist Frederick's clinic. She was quite anxious, but now she thought that she would open with Athena's kidnapping in her dreams.

When she met Frederick, she realised that he is the one who can save Athena and punish the real culprit. She was sure of her dream, as it was disclosed now, still it is quite a mystery to her.

Again, the scientist told her the same process of choosing the dream. "Imagine the dream image, it reaches your desired scene." He gave her a dream journal and told her to monitor the place, signs, characters, and events in the dream. He said, "When you get around the dream, write down everything you envisioned, it will reveal the exact picture." It was a challenge for Stephanie to remember its clear picture.

Sometimes Stephanie finds no words to express her dream; she struggles as the ability to remember flees away. She sleeps eight hours every day, but scientists feel that she is creating resistance to remember her dream somehow.

Frederick asked her, "Jot down your mood when you get up."

— what you saw?

Where have you seen her?

Who were the people who were taking Athena?

When were they abducting her?

These questions, when answered by you, will be a quick line for me to reach the conclusion stage.

If you saw any picture... draw!

If any written word... journal

If you hear any voices... listen, use small note cards.

Finally, in the second stage, the scientist has done the dream-digging activity. He studied the symbols, places, and scenes which she mentioned in the journal. He asked her to touch the image and clarify if she had seen them in real life. He told her to audio record what she envisioned in the dream. He asked her umpteen times to jot in the journal and memorise the dream.

He provided her dream kit with a dream bag. It was a beautiful bag with a girl sitting on a bed, a journal, a dream pillow, and flower fragrance essence for oneiric vision therapy.

Scientist Frederick has a dream dictionary where there were dream symbols interpretation. It is a book of database arranged from A to Z. He searched in it, and he started getting clarity about symbols and characters.

Last stage was consulting his team. Stephanie's dual personality was subdued through this process.

I met myself in a dream.

I remember the fragrance of my soul.

The touch of my heart,

The breath of my life,

My voice reverberates in my ears.

Singing to open wide to share
Myself with the world!
I met myself in a dream.
She wrote the above lines in her journal during her visit
to the scientist's clinic.

CHAPTER TEN

EMILY'S FATHER JAMES WAS MURDERED

It was declared as a suicide by his two business partners. The dream uncovers the true mystery. Scientist Frederick walks into her dream and finds the secret beneath. He asks Emily to drink the dream formula which reveals the hidden truth. James wants to share through his recurring presence in Emily's dream that his partners were drug dealers who supplied drugs to various parts of the country.

The office premises have an underground area used as an orphanage for kids, which was not known to James. Scientist Frederick envisions the dream of an Emily to gather information from it. Her father has something mysterious to disclose in her dream. James was pointing towards a mysterious object (a knife) near the fruit bowl. Not only was he murdered, but he was also a victim of a plot played by his business partners. He mentioned the names of the business partners who were involved in this murder.

Emily told the scientist, "In my dream, my father was moving towards his office room, as he forgot to bring the keys of the car. He approached the room; he heard a loud voice coming out of the room. At one instance, he just moved towards the window to hear what conversation it is about!"

They were discussing how to transfer the location of the drug dealing warehouse to another place. Her father knew that they supplied powdered medicines for pharmaceuticals and hired a small group of children for packing. They provided food and shelter to these kids at night.

He heard that it is not an orphanage, but rather a headquarters for the supply of drugs. In the night when the whole world sleeps, illegal activities like trafficking of children occur. It was a great shock to his father when he heard this conversation. He immediately went inside the room, causing both partners to understand that he knows the truth.

Her father argued and asked them to surrender to the police department, but they disagreed. Within a few minutes, they decided to clear their path, so they pulled the knife and inserted it inside his body. No one was there; the children were downstairs in the underground, so it was easy for both partners to change the whole scenario of the murder. Her father tried hard to save himself, but in the end, as the knife was inserted, he fell to the ground.

Scientist Frederick took the help of his dream team Parker, the Dream Catcher, and Roger, the Dream Weaver. Also, Sam, the Dream Architect, created nightmares in the partners' dreams instead of pleasant dreams, which made them anxious and agitated to reveal the truth.

The secret uncovered that the building was not helping orphans and abandoned children; it was a racket of child trafficking. Small girls were conveyed to different countries for the sake of monetary benefit. It was a deceit under the veil of kindness and care.

Several children were sent to different countries to sell drugs illegally with a begging task, so that the agents' true intentions remain hideous. Both partners were actively involved with foreign agents, but her father has no idea of this secret.

Her father's first reaction is shocking when he heard this conversation. He was misled as the orphanage building was in the combined name of all three partners. Emily and her mother could not believe their ears when the truth came out. The scientist told them the whole incident which was related to Emily's dream.

Emily fainted but later, realised as her mother comforted her that her father was a noble, honest person who was protected from the veil of false accusations.

Scientist Frederick's formula helps Emily to come out of this deceit and betrayal which was enticed by her father's business partners. Her father's case was initiated and soon they were penalised for their crime under severe law enforcement.

Emily after her last dream counselling process thanked the scientist. He gave a beautiful dream book to her. She was grateful to the scientist for the dream evaluation. Emily was satisfied that the real culprits faced consequences as the truth came out with her father's proof of no offence.

CHAPTER ELEVEN

BREAKDOWN OF THE ACTUAL PLAN

Patrick's dream was not clear, but Scientist Frederick and his team put forth earnest effort to break the strategy of robber Jeffery. Patrick saw a plot in the dream but forgot it as he woke up; just a glimpse remains in his mind.

The plan includes pulling the workers who come monthly for the repair of the computerised (electro-digital) lock system, as the team does not comprise maintenance workers. They trained their team for the repairing task. The heist was planned so that they will disable the locking system.

Patrick saw the dream and mentioned what he remembered in the dream. It was a challenge for him to find the full strategy and confirm with higher departments to prevent the heist.

Day Thursday 25th October was the day planned for the heist, when they would be entering the premises of the World Bank as maintenance boys to repair the digitalised locking system. They knew how to create a fake code in the system and break the real code; only two people were allowed to enter the main premises of the World Bank.

No one outside was allowed to get inside without permission. The locking system was scanned and disabled a few minutes ago by those people.

They reach the place wearing face masks so that their visibility was uncovered. High-security personnel allowed them as maintenance personnel. It took twenty minutes for them to break the code, and they were given permission to disguise the treasury transfer to the security truck standing outside the bank. Then suddenly alarms all over started beeping with high volume as an alert for all security guards. All the lights were closed, but due to the beeping, all the guards gathered near the main locker room gate.

Scientist Frederick understood the code 2369 through Patrick's dream, and he informed the security system to make a change in the code in the binary locking system. Jeffery thought that his gang was able to break the code; instead, the locking alarm started functioning to prevent any heist. Scientist Frederick mentioned the whole picture to the Chief Safety Officer and Minister of External Affairs. They asked their team to recreate the lock system.

Jeffrey and the gang were smart people, so they were able to break that code as well, but they could not take out the treasury as they found it empty, from the World Bank premises. The treasury had been moved to a secure place, and the locker was emptied one day before the heist.

As the alarm started, they were startled and tried to run away through a hidden passage but were caught by the high-security staff, so the plan failed.

Patrick thanked the scientist as he was the one who was able to fulfil his dream. Patrick was awarded a special prize named "Superhero" by the state minister.

Roger, Sam, and Parker curated Jeffrey and the gang's dream, and they were forced to work according to the initial heist plan. When Patrick drank the formula, Scientist Frederick walked into Patrick's dream and found the code of the treasury. A new code was constructed through Sam, the Dream Architect, in Jeffrey's dream.

Dream Alchemist Barner found the strategy of the heist. Patrick was so happy to share this news with his friends, and they planned a party for the "Superhero Award."

CHAPTER TWELVE

REAL CULPRIT WAS DETECTED!!

Scientist Frederick discerned who the real culprit of Athena's kidnapping was. Last few days he started assessing the feelings of Stephanie. He asked several questions to her.

"How do you feel when you are ready to sleep?"

"How do you feel in a dream?"

"What do you feel when you get into the deeper aspects of a dream?"

He found out that the dream was rich in symbols. She mentioned the whereabouts of the kidnapping place.

Scientist Frederick gave her a drink of a magic formula to visualise the culprit of the oneiric kidnapping as the last stage. He walked into Stephanie's dream to confirm that Athena was kidnapped, not just a notion of hers.

Stephanie described the incident as what she saw "a daily routine she was going with her to Athena's house. Her mother swiftly moved towards the workplace, but due to a thorn prick in her leg, she was left behind.

Athena came out of her house near the lane to grab the bus. Suddenly, three people in a car rushed towards her and put her in the car. Nobody was outside the house. Stephanie just saw the face of one person who was the house help to them.

Stephanie shouted to protect, but she was at a distance from the incident place. Athena too was crying initially, but due to the cloth on her face, her voice could not be heard. All the kidnappers were in a hurry with their faces covered, but in haste, one person's mask fell off, which led to the identification of the culprit by Stephanie in a dream.

"They were behaving badly with her. I ran towards my mother when they left to tell my truth, but my mother silenced me and told me that they will not believe you; instead, they will think that you too were involved. Stephanie forced her mother to talk clearly about the incident, but they took Stephanie's words lightly."

After two days, through dream interpretation and evaluation by Scientist Frederick Parker, the Dream Catcher, and Katie, the dream detective, identified and traced Calvin, the servant of the house who has been working for twenty years, as the culprit of this crime. The scientist told the police department to catch the real kidnapper. Finally, the police department found Athena within a few hours near a dark and isolated room adjacent to the lake where they had kept her for ransom and their desires. All the kidnappers were arrested and punished.

Stephanie was so happy as she was provided with higher studies fees from Athena's parents. She gave a handmade teddy bear and a drawing book to Athena to cheer her up and forget about this awful incident. After this incident, Stephanie's condition improved as her mother consulted doctors for her dual personality disorder and gave her proper treatment, which led her to become a confident personality.

Scientist and the team, along with Stephanie, were also published in a newspaper highlight as they caught hold of Calvin and other kidnappers with their dream team. Frederick realised that his team is required at every stage; sometimes when the dream evaluation process is midway, we need teamwork to analyse the whole scenario and reach the endpoint of the dream evaluation journey. He appreciated his team for uncovering the hidden secret of Emily, preventing the heist of the World Bank, and criminal identification with unflinching support and unfailing enthusiasm.

He unravelled the mystery of Emily, Patrick, and Stephanie's dream journey.

CHAPTER THIRTEEN

BACK TO THE EVENT

The hall was beaming with the sound of beats all around the stage, with the shrieking sound of clapping. Scientist Frederick came back from his flashback.

A child with a disability was singing a beautiful song, standing behind his mother who was supporting him. After the various programmes, the hunt for the Biggest Dreamer Award started.

Scientist started writing the names of contestants to declare the results.

The top contestants are:

Samuel Wilson -He is a person with artistic hand who painted sublime landmark paintings. He is blind but no one can guess when they see his paintings, as there is not a slight trace of painting created by person without vision. Due to vision problem, he has no idea of colour, but his creations were so full of vivid colours and expressions.

From his childhood, he was fascinated with the art of paintings, as his elder sister used to describe and explain the various forms of paintings. It was his dream to create his own art gallery with paintings of distinct colour combinations and abstract compositions. His figures in myriad paintings were so mesmerising and creative that every figure has a unique story to tell. Every painting emanates a visual expression with brush strokes of varied colours, shapes, and textures.

He wants people to visit his art gallery. His dream was to receive the Best Painter Award. He works day and night and hones his skill to achieve this award. His journey started with numerous ebbs and flows as he had no mentor to ignite his spirit. Despite many struggles with poverty along with his blindness, he was able to pursue his dream. On New Year's Eve, he was awarded the 'Best Painter' award by the President of the country. It is a miracle for him as he has no idea about colours, brushes, and canvas, yet he painted with a unique perspective. Not only does he depict stories exquisitely in his paintings, but the colours are also apt, and his art evokes a feeling of appreciation in those who view the paintings.

It was an arduous task for the scientist to select him as one of the special contestants for the Dreamer Award. He was in tears when he noticed his stupendous painting and his affection towards its creativity.

When he heard the true story of how he reached his destination of receiving the "Best Painter Award" by the President of the country, he put a tick next to one of the awardees of the show.

CHAPTER FOURTEEN

HUNT CONTINUES!!

Second Contestant is Eddie Smith, who was extremely poor as there was no one to support him for his education, an immense burden on him to earn a livelihood. His father died at an early stage, and they reside in a remote area of the country where there were no proper sanitation and health facilities, no proper drainage system, and no adequate transportation facility.

Eddie was an intelligent and curious child from his childhood. His small-town guide was always amused by his intellectual questions. He had two sisters who were supported by his mother for living. He resided with his family in the charitable institute which provided food and shelter. Although his mother went to work in others' houses for cleaning and household work, still the income earned by his mother was insufficient to rear the three children.

When he was six years old, a ray of hope emerged; a missionary institution personnel visited their place for a project. They came to hold a seminar on sanitation in that area. Eddie was playing nearby, and as he got inside the hall and listened to the speech quietly. He was curious by nature, so when he heard the speech, he asked a few questions related to the topic. The team members were astonished by his enthusiasm. They decided to provide support for his education and training. It opened a world of opportunities; he was longing for this moment to change his destiny.

Gradually, by his diligence, he scored good marks in his educational institute. Eddie passed exams with flying colours. Later, in college, he conducted numerous scientific experiments and created apparatus by his skill and innovative ideas. Finally, he got a doctorate in Physics. With further advancement in his career during his professional tenure, he was awarded "Best Physicist" by the country forum. He also received "Pioneer Physics Inventor."

One can imagine, without proper food and shelter facilities, still, by his interest and inquisitiveness, he touched the skies in his field and fulfilled his dream. Scientist Frederick, when he heard of his struggles, started imagining how he too encompasses a hard life and alleviated the financial strain of his family. He clapped as he listened to his story and was startled by how his dream let him grow amidst challenges and achieve his goals.

CHAPTER FIFTEEN

GUESS THE THIRD CONTESTANT?

Scientist Frederick ticked the names of the first and second contestants. For further approval, he passed the list to other judges. He laid a finger on the list and waited to hear about the third contestant.

Henry Brown, who could not see injustice from his childhood, was a medium-height fellow with a vibrant personality, brown eyes, an oval face, and a little beard on his jawline. One can imagine him as the leader for his rights.

When he was small, he used to stand up against elders bullying small kids. He cannot bear injustice at any cost. He always stands for the right notion. He remains true to his word even though he was punished for speaking the truth. He was vehemently against the cruelty of foreigners towards his compatriots. Foreigners invaded his country; they treated the people brutally.

In his college days, he started a movement for protection against the atrocities done by foreigners on fellow beings. He was put in jail; there his liver was damaged due to adverse conditions in jail, but still he survived. He created a large group of supporters for his joint mission to fight against injustice. He devoted all his time to protecting the rights of his people. He stands as a beacon of inspiration and a pillar of strength for his people.

He revolted against the invaders. In chill and high fever, he stood for his people and attended various rallies. He went to jail numerous times. He used to dream of being a standout leader for his country. Henry wants to work for the better ment by creating laws to safeguard the interest of the public. He conducted several events and marches to break their hostility.

Soon, he became the hero among the masses as his party fought a legal battle to throw out these foreigners from the country, but his health sometimes did not allow him to withstand long rallies and agitation as he had asthma and a major chronic disease. With his and his team's effort, finally, their country got independence.

An idol who withstands hardships to put his foot forward, he was known as a pioneer for standing against injustice and was honoured by the Head of the country. He was appointed as a minister of the country. His story reminds the new generation that strong battles cannot hinder freedom but rather create lasting change in their lives.

Scientist Frederick, when he listened to his life story, gave a standing gesture, and realised that not even physical health problems could dismay him. He remains a pillar of strength for his countrymen, protecting the interests of his country's people.

CHAPTER SIXTEEN

The Excitement Continues

Scientist Frederick moved towards the name of the next contestant.

Fiona Green, who was awarded best-selling author of the year, walked towards the stage. One could see the exuberant personality with both hands beside her back, moving swiftly to tell the story to the audience.

She began her life path. She is endowed with creativity, and she creates stories from her childhood. She used to narrate stories to her friends by giving them moral lessons whenever they played with her. She dreamed of being the best author when she grew up.

Once, when she went to attend her family function by train, the mishap occurred, due to which she lost both hands. She was ten years old at that time when this accident took place. She got injured, lost both her hands, and later found it difficult to use them in the future.

Fiona's fondness towards creating stories led her to find a different path. She used both legs for writing. She took help from her sister to support her in the journey of writing. Her sister could not help her as she had to leave for further studies to a distant place.

Initially, it was a challenging task to hold the pen with her legs, but later, with her willpower and continuous effort, she developed the steps to write with her legs. She used her leg fingers to grip the pen to write.

She pens down several splendid stories of humanity, love, friendship, and inspiration. She excels in her field as her stories touch the hearts of people. Her creativity is so mesmerising that the readers end up reading the whole story and learn small lessons.

The stories enlightened the masses with beautiful messages embedded in them. The messages were for everyone to stand against adversity and to create their own heroic world.

Fiona Green took a few months to come to a normal life after the accident but fought her battle against these challenges, surpassed them and came out with a bang of awards and achievements. She uses innovative technologies to create magic with words and build a place in the hearts of thousands of people in her country. She has the calibre to tap into writing skills to navigate complex situations. She connects with people through empathy and understanding.

Frederick was astonished at how a dream can bloom even in unforeseen circumstances and heard about the wonderful journey of fulfilling her dream.

CHAPTER SEVENTEEN

A Technocrat Innovator

Technology is the need of the hour. At any phase, we need it whether it is in commodities, services, clothing, or health; it is required everywhere.

Hannah Collins devised a programme to curate new advancements in space technology and innovate new methods and ideas to help the masses. She did her graduation from just a normal college but after working hard for further studies, she earned her master's degree in computers to upskill in technology. She developed a gadget for medical purposes which, when worn, can detect diseases. She excels in her field. Hannah introduced technological branding products. Soon she got married and gave birth to twins, Amelia, and Olivia.

They were pretty and ebullient girls. Her dream to achieve "The Best Technocrat" was demolished when she got married. Soon as a mother, she started shouldering household responsibilities for long hours to rear her children.

Both her daughters, Amelia, and Olivia grew up with the dream to shine. Amelia wants to become a space astronaut to revolutionise space travel, while Olivia wants to create a comic character for children. Amelia, an amateur pioneer, was the first female to fly solo, breaking the barriers of Aviation and Space travel. Olivia's dream was to inspire children through acting in plays and creating numerous fictional characters. She created the world of dreamland with her imaginative iconic characters. Soon her theatrical performances made her the best actor for fictional characters.

The list of dreamers included all three names: Hannah Collins - the mother, Amelia the space astronaut, and Olivia - creator of comic characters for children.

When both the daughters' dreams became their reality, Hannah opened a centre to help the people fulfil their dreams. Her innovation has wings to fly high, a mission to support, and a vision to excel leading to new horizons. A big unit to teach and innovate technological ideas and systems was initiated to create awareness and build a foundation for the future. It is not an individual triumph; rather, it is a collaborative initiative to transform generations.

It was a great achievement for her as her innovative classes, products, and system became the best brand in the country, providing work for the younger generation, technological output, and incentives to grow in the field.

CHAPTER EIGHTEEN

A Visionary Entrepreneur

Charlotte Brookes' name was announced as the last contestant for the event. Now, she is a visionary entrepreneur, but her initial years were full of financial challenges. She had a poverty-ridden family with no parents to support her. She studied in a missionary school where education was free. She used to work in the library to arrange books and maintain the daily register. Charlotte got $10 for this task per month.

Charlotte saves every penny after household expenses for her future goals. Her ambition knows no bounds. She has an innovative mindset. She is confident about implementing her idea. Charlotte invested in a money-saving scheme from her initial stage, which was supported by her teacher.

Later, she started taking classes for small children. Gradually, with the passage of time, she opened a coaching institute. Charlotte mortgaged a house that was meant to provide food and shelter to the needy kids. With growing income, she started developing courses to incorporate her ideas. "

She initiated a start-up in which her sister Marie, used to stitch bags made of waste material. It was a small project, but as time passed, she was funded with a government scheme.

She ventured into a store managed by her sister, Isabella. Meanwhile, they opened a cloud kitchen that supplies food to nearby residents. As her repertoire expanded, the bag store became the talk of the town; more people approached, and the store extended to five more cities, which were run by her loved ones.

When she was in college, she also learned the art of manufacturing beauty products. It was in the store displays that she included beauty products with the brand name 'Beauty,' which was a tremendous success. Her profit margin doubled every year with constant hard work and a dream to be a big entrepreneur. Soon she ascended to fame with her grit, diligence, and multitasking skills.

The scientist, when he heard about her advancement, felt she was a simple girl with a mere financial background. Still, she became one of the richest people in the country as she dreamed to be big and worked accordingly to achieve it. He was astonished to learn about her success and dream fulfilment story.

FINAL COUNTDOWN!!

Scientist Frederick cannot move his eyes from these amazing dream contestants. It was just fifteen minutes left to announce the result. There was a stand-up comedian 'Mr Smith,' a dynamic and astounding personality who was invited for emceeing the ceremony.

The crowd burst into laughter as they heard the jokes and outspoken reality bites full of humour. He spoke few words which mentioned world disasters in a hilarious way. Fredrick too was engrossed with this comedy performance.

Meanwhile, the judges together discussed the winning contestants. The criteria for selection were at the final stage to announce the winner, first runner-up, and second runner-up, along with a few other categories.

Finally, the moment arrived for which the audience had been waiting for such a long time. Scientist Frederick moved towards the stage with the fellow chief guest to honour the Biggest Dreamer award.

Countdown begins!!

Scientist Frederick said, "Everyone is fond of their dream to live and fulfil them. It is a garland of flowers which surrounds us and spreads its fragrance. Our dream is sweet of happiness, a dip of contentment, a bite of serenity whose taste lingers all over our mind. We can live through this magic wand which gives us an ambition to grow and hope to rise. It is an output of our inputs given by our subconscious mind. Let us find out who is the biggest dreamer who tastes the bite of dreamland."

"Any guesses? Come on! Start listing!"

The Biggest Dreamer Award goes to Fiona Greens and Samuel Wilson; they both share the Biggest Dreamer award.

First Runner-Up to "Hannah Collins" and Second Runner is "Henry Brown."

Fiona Greens and Samuel Wilson won the Best Biggest Dreamer Award as both overcame challenges, though with their disabilities excel in their domain with grit and resilience.

Hannah Collins was awarded as the First Runner-Up Biggest Dreamer Award as she stood for others and laid the foundation for fulfilling the future generation's dream. She sacrificed her life for her daughters. With so many challenges, she opened a technological school for coming generations. It depicts compassion and a desire to make a difference in others' lives.

Henry Brown got the Runner-Up Second Biggest Dreamer Award for standing against the injustice, and with his arduous efforts, his country gained independence from foreigners.

Eddie Smith was bestowed with the Visionary Dreamer Award as he discovered several laws and apparatus that are beneficial for the future scientific world and the further enhancement of scientific studies.

CHAPTER TWENTY

CHERISH YOUR DREAMS

Scientist Frederick and fellow judges applauded the winners. He asked his teammates to come on stage, and he shared a message with everyone:

Always dream big.

You will dig deep,

A Goldmine will crop,

To give you a thousand leaps

To shine and reap!

Everyone greeted the winners, and trophies were given to awardees.

The scientist concluded his speech with a beautiful description of a dream.

"Dream is a joy

Dream is a Pain,

Dream is embedded beauty.

Dream is a lesson to learn,

to grow, to survive,

to discover! To be free!!"

Dear readers! Are you satisfied by Scientist Frederick and the fellow chief guests' decision? Do mention in my email (preeti.agarwal73@gmail.com)

There is certain terminology which comes across when you read my book.

1. Oneiric: Pertains to dreams

2. Oneirology: Study of dreams

3. Oneirocritics: Dream Interpreter

5.Oneiros: To dream

6. Mantic Alphabets: The alphabets used for prediction of the future.

Let us catch the train of a dream journey, which is exciting and magical!

Cherish your dreams!

Cherish the focus attached to it!

Cherish the beauty inside it!

There are certain affirmations for happy dreaming before you go to bed.

1. I love and accept myself.

2. I attract positivity, happiness, love, peace, and abundance in my life.

3. My dreams support me in every way.

4. I release in my dreams that hurt me in any form to manifest real joy in my life.

5. My dream is filled with pleasant experiences.

What you see,

What you want is a dream,

It causes the frequency to vibrate.

And that frequency is transmitted to your dreams.

So, my readers!

Crack the codes of your dreams to create the world of happiness,

The everlasting joy that constitutes a concrete structure.

www.ingramcontent.com/pod-product-compliance
Lightning Source LLC
Chambersburg PA
CBHW020651160726
47991CB00003B/1135